C016939401

Nicola Davies
Pretend Cows

Illustrations Cathy Fisher

GRAFFEG

Pretend Cows

Maxy sat high up in the biggest apple tree. Mrs Bunting was calling her in to have her tea.

'Maxine! Maxine!' she squeaked.

Maxy chewed thoughtfully on a grass stem and wondered how such a teeny voice could come from such a big, fat body.

Mrs Bunting was getting really cross.

'Maxine! I *know* you can hear me. Come in here *at once!*'

Maxy *was* hungry, and she *did* like Mrs B's teas – lovely gravy and brilliant roast potatoes. But she didn't want to come down from her tree.

At last, the kitchen door slammed. Mrs Bunting had given up. She got into her little car and rattled over the bumps in the farmyard and up the lane, home to give Mr Bunting his tea.

Maxy sighed and leant her cheek against the trunk. It was covered in moss, soft and furry, almost like a teddy. It was comforting to be held in the arms of the tree, up above everything. She could look down on the farm and pretend that it still *was* a proper farm, with cows in the milking parlour and pigs in the sties. But down on the ground she noticed the silence too much, the empty barns, the lost-looking house.

There were no animals on Stelly Farm anymore. All the cows and pigs had been killed, shot by vets and soldiers, and then piled in a heap and burned. Daddy had said it had to be done because they *might* be sick and then *might* make animals on neighbouring farms sick too. Maxy couldn't understand it. Anyone could see that all their animals were fine! She wanted to tell the vets that they were wrong, but on the day they came, Mum and Dad sent her away to Nan's.

She had ridden an old bike round and round and round Nan's tiny garden until it got dark and Nan had made her come inside. The next day, when Nan took her home, the yard had been hosed and the barns swept; there wasn't a trace of an animal to be seen. Even their smell faded after a while. Maxy snuffled in corners to find the last familiar whiffs of pig or cow.

Dad had to work away after that, milking a big herd of cows belonging to a farmer on the other side of the county. He left before Maxy woke and often got back after she was asleep. Mum worked harder too, cycling off down the lane to the village every morning to clean people's houses. Sometimes Maxy went to Nan's after school, and sometimes Mrs Bunting came and cooked her tea and squeaked around the kitchen until Mum got home.

Everything was sad without the animals and the daily

routine of feeding and milking. Moping round the empty farm was boring, so Maxy found a way to make herself feel better: Pretend Cows. She would walk out into the fields and bring the herd of Pretend Cows into the yard, ready for milking, just as she'd done with the real ones. It felt nice to shout the names of her old favourites and to scold them like she used to do.

'C'mon, Patch, pick your feet up. That's my gal, Ella. Get on there, Daze!'

In some ways, Pretend Cows were better than real ones, because Pretend Cows only needed attention when the weather was fine.

Sometimes, when the Pretend Cows were being milked, Maxy would stand at the door of the milking parlour. She'd imagine the *shlump, shlump, shlump* of the milking machine and the sound of her dad singing along to the radio as he worked.

Little by little, things began to get a bit better. Dad got a job nearer the farm and sometimes came home for tea. He began to talk about 'restocking', buying new animals and starting again. At Christmas, Mum and Dad talked about 'making plans' and smiled secretly at each other over the turkey. At Easter, they told her that she would be having a little brother or sister in the summer. Maxy told them that was OK but that she'd rather have cows and pigs on the farm than a baby. Mum and Dad laughed, and Mum said that maybe by the summer they'd have a baby *and* animals!

When spring came all the Pretend Cows had twins, and there was even a Pretend Pig and ten Pretend Piglets in the end sty. Things were definitely looking up! But then Mum got ill and had to go to hospital, and Maxy started living up the apple tree.

Maxy woke in Dad's arms. He was carrying her down the ladder, out of the tree.

'Why can't I sleep up there?' she whined sleepily.

'Because you're not a monkey. Now don't wriggle, else we'll both fall!'

It was cold now. The sky was streaked with purple and dotted with the first stars. Maxy let Dad hold her tight and carry her right across the yard and into the warm kitchen.

He dolloped her into a chair, wrapped in his sweater.

'Mmmm. Mrs Bunting's teas!' he said. 'Want some?'

Maxy nodded. The gravy was a bit crusty round the edges, but it still tasted good. Dad and Maxy ate it all up.

'Ahh,' said Dad, leaning back in his chair. 'That's better! So, what did you do after school today?'

'Milking, of course!' Maxy said. How could Dad forget that? It amazed her. Dad looked at the floor and ran one hand through his hair. It didn't do any good, Maxy noticed,

it stayed just as spiky and wild as ever.

'Oh,' he sighed. 'The pretend cows again.'

'Yes. The cows,' said Maxy, sticking out her chin. 'Milk yield's down and Stella's limping badly on her right hind foot. But we don't need the vet because I put a poultice on it earlier!'

Dad opened his mouth to say something, then shut it again.

'Is there any pudding?' asked Maxy.

She ate one slice of pie and Dad ate two, and almost all the custard. Then they sat together and listened to the bubbling sound the range always made at night.

After a while, Dad cleared his throat and said, 'I went to see Mum tonight, Maxy.'

Maxy knew he'd been to the hospital because he'd changed out of his work overalls and put on a clean shirt, but she didn't say anything. 'D'you want to know how she was?'

Maxy looked up at the ceiling. She didn't want to look at Dad. He might say Mum was all right, but that couldn't be true because she was in hospital.

Maxy looked harder at the ceiling: there was a crack around the light fitting that looked just like a drawing of a wing or the edge of a pie or perhaps a beehive.

'She's much better, Maxy,' Dad's voice went on. 'And the

baby's very nearly ready to be born!'

He sounded really excited, but Maxy still didn't want to look at him. Dad *said* it was OK. But it might not be, and Maxy didn't want to think about that at all. That was why she had never been to see Mum in hospital. So she stared straight at the light bulb. At first it was white, then yellow, and then a kind of blobby pink, filling up her eyes and burning everything else away.

'I'm going to bed now, Dad,' Maxy said. 'I need to be up early to look at that poultice.'

The next day, Nan picked Maxy up from school. She said that Dad had taken an afternoon off and was waiting for her at home!

Maxy didn't say anything. Nan was sure to be wrong, she was always getting in a muddle about things. Mrs Bunting would be waiting, not Dad. So Maxy made plans to check on the Pretend Cows and then to scoot up the apple tree.

But Nan was right. Dad was in the yard, busy putting the finishing touches to a new chicken coop.

'What's that for?' Maxy asked.

'Bantams,' Dad said. 'You know, Maxy, little chickens. Good layers, and good broodies too.'

'Why?'

'I thought some proper fresh eggs would be good for your

mum and the baby.'

Maxy walked all around the coop. Dad had done a great job. There was a little house at one end with a sloping tin roof and a door that slid open when you pulled a string. There was a box at the back of the house, with a lid to lift to collect the eggs, and a run at the front covered in wire to give the bantams a safe place to scratch about.

Dad nailed a latch onto the lid of the egg box.

'That's it. It's ready. Will you help me carry it, Max?'

'I don't know,' Maxy said. 'It's nearly time to bring the cows in.'

'I know, but this won't take a minute. We can put it on the grass by the apple tree.'

Maxy took the light end, and they carried the coop across the yard together.

'Which way round would the chickens like best?' Maxy asked.

'I'm not sure. What do you think?'

Maxy thought for a minute.

'They'd like the morning sun, so they can warm up quick if it's been cold at night.'

'Good idea,' said Dad. 'So they should face the house?'

Maxy nodded.

'When will you get the chickens?'

'Oh,' said Dad. 'Pretty soon.'

Ha! Maxy knew what *that* meant! He'd been saying the same thing for months about when they'd be getting some more cows. Maxy glared at him, but he didn't seem to notice.

'Hadn't you better check on Stella's bad leg?' he said, with a big smile. Dad never asked about the Pretend Cows, he was just trying to get rid of her so she wouldn't ask about the stupid bantams anymore. She didn't bother to tell him that Stella was fine now, and had given birth to triplets!

She turned and ran off into the first field, calling, 'Stella! Daze! Marty! C'mon now!'

The Pretend Cows were behaving very badly.

The calves kept running off, and even the grown-ups were skittish and wouldn't go where Maxy wanted them to. Maxy gave up. Might as well be up the apple tree, she thought.

Just as she got within sight of the tree, a very loud noise came from Dad's coop. 'Cooockkodddooodleoooooooo!'

Maxy raced up to take a closer look. There, strutting in the new run, as if he'd owned it *forever*, was a perfect little cockerel! He had glossy chestnut feathers that flashed purple and blue where they caught the light. They were brightest at his throat, where they shone and billowed like a silk scarf, and on his tail, where they shot up like a rainbow fountain. Maxy could see that he knew how beautiful he was. He swaggered up and down the run, tossing his head

and making his bright red comb flop over one eye.

Dad came and stood beside her.

'I didn't know soon was now!' said Maxy.

Dad grinned. 'What should we call him?' he asked.

Maxy thought of an old pop star she'd seen on TV once, someone who'd been famous even before Dad was born. He'd wiggled just like this cockerel and had a floppy fringe like the cockerel's droopy comb.

'Elvis!' said Maxy. 'That's his name!'

Dad laughed out loud and ruffled her hair with his hand.

'Well, let's see if Elvis likes the wives I've got him.'

He reached into the cardboard box at his feet and pulled out a squawking bundle of feathers, which he shoved, quickly, into the run through the little door at its end.

The bundle turned out to be three hens, bunched up together. They stepped apart and shook their feathers. Two of them reminded Maxy of Nan's tea cosy. They were round and homely, with soft fluffy feathers that looked like fur. One was brown and the other was white, but they both had a spot of blue skin on their cheeks, like a tiny patch of sky.

'They're silkies,' said Dad. 'Your mum kept silkies when she was a girl. They're the best mums. They sit tight on their eggs no matter what, until they hatch.'

'What'll we call them?' Maxy asked.

'Coffee and Cream?' said Dad.

Maxy nodded.

Elvis started showing off to Coffee and Cream immediately. Maxy could see that they were only pretending to ignore him. But the third hen really was ignoring all Elvis's fine feathers and strutting about. She stood at the end of the run and stared up into the branches of the apple tree.

'She's a cross-breed,' said Dad. 'Her mum was a partridge Wyandotte but her dad was a duckwinged Old English Game.'

Maxy nodded as if she knew all about wire-pots and duck-games. Whatever she was, Maxy liked the look of the third hen. There was nothing rounded or fluffy about her at all. She had long legs and smooth grey feathers that fitted her closely. She had proper wings too, with long black feathers, folded neatly to her sides. Her eyes were bright and her comb was small and tidy, like a cap. She looked ready for anything.

'Her eggs will be pretty tiny,' said Dad. 'But she was free, so I'm not grumbling! What d'you want to call her?'

'I don't know yet. I'll have to get to know her a bit.'

'Fair enough,' said Dad.

Dad filled the chickens' special water holder from the tap in the yard and fetched layers' pellets for them from the feed store where they used to keep the cows' food. Then he and Maxy stood with the afternoon sun on their backs, watching the four birds get used to their new home.

Elvis and the two silkies were settling in together nicely, pecking from the feeder and taking turns to sip water. But the third hen had turned her back on them and was pacing up and down the run. She didn't look very happy.

'Don't worry,' Dad said. 'She'll feel at home once she's laid an egg here!'

But Maxy wasn't so sure.

'I'm going to keep watch, to make sure she's all right,' said Maxy. 'From up the tree.'

Dad sighed. He looked disappointed.

'Will you come down for supper?' he asked.

'Maybe,' said Maxy.

The next morning there was a note on the kitchen table, written on the back of an old envelope with one of Maxy's crayons, a pink one.

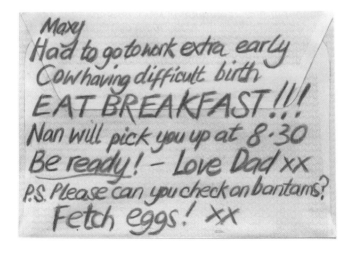

Maxy
Had to go to work extra early
Cow having difficult birth
EAT BREAKFAST!!!
Nan will pick you up at 8·30
Be ready! – Love Dad xx
P.S. Please can you check on bantams?
Fetch eggs! xx

It was a lovely warm morning. The sun was shining right on the chicken coop. Looking out of the kitchen window, Maxy could see the bantams scratching about already. She put her cereal into a big mug, to make it easy to carry, got a spoon from the drawer and headed outside to have breakfast with the chickens.

Elvis, Coffee and Cream clucked hopefully when she sat down on the grass by the coop. They knew that human visitors meant easy food. They watched her through the mesh for a few moments, but when they worked out she wasn't going to share her cereal, they went back to pecking their pellets.

It took Maxy a moment to spot the third hen (she still hadn't thought of a name for her); she was dust-bathing in a little dip of bare earth. Her feathers were ruffled, fluffed out, so that she looked soft and scruffy. She rolled and shuffled, so that the dusty earth flew up around her and caught the light like gold, but when she saw Maxy watching her, she popped up onto her skinny legs and shook herself smooth. Maxy didn't know if hens could be embarrassed, but she certainly looked as though she was.

The hen began scratching furiously at the ground then staring fiercely at the place she'd disturbed, looking for worms. She found one almost at once; it writhed in her beak, looking as big as a snake against her tiny body.

It looked far too much for the hen to swallow, but she managed it, gulping hard and squeezing her bright eyes tight shut in concentration. At last, the worm was gone. Maxy thought the hen looked a bit sick, like someone who'd eaten two of Mrs Bunting's teas. But a moment later she chased a fat bluebottle around the run and leapt like a goalie going for a save to catch it in her beak. Maxy wanted to cheer.

Watching the hen was so interesting that Maxy didn't hear Nan's car pull into the yard, and only noticed her when she sat down on the grass.

'Hi,' said Nan. 'Nice chooks! What's that little one called?'

'I don't know,' sighed Maxy. 'I can't decide. She's too fierce and clever for an ordinary name.'

'Minerva,' said Nan. 'She was the goddess of wisdom, Greek or Roman or something; I don't recall. Anyway, dead clever.'

'Minerva. OK,' said Maxy. 'I like it!'

Nan smiled and got up. 'Good,' she said. 'OK, Maxy. Time to go!'

'Wait!' said Maxy. 'I forgot about the eggs!'

She ran to the nest box at the back of the pen and gently lifted the lid. Nestling in the straw were two white eggs. They were a bit smaller than normal hens' eggs, but plump and cosy-looking; just the sort of eggs you'd expect the fluffy

silkies to lay! Maxy looked for Minerva's egg; it would be really small, and quite pointy too, she thought. But there was nothing. In spite of dust-bathing and worm-swallowing, the little chicken didn't feel at home enough to lay.

The good weather didn't last the day. By the time Nan dropped Maxy off after school it was blustery, cold and raining. Mrs Bunting was waiting in the yard with an umbrella. She took Maxy's hand and marched her to the kitchen door.

'You're not climbing up trees with a storm brewing, young lady. A good tea is what you need.'

Maxy didn't bother arguing. She sat at the table while Mrs Bunting clattered saucepans on the range, then put the plate of food in front of her. It was her favourite, lamb with buttery carrots, roast potatoes and Mrs Bunting's lovely gravy. Maxy suddenly felt very bad about hiding up the tree so many times.

'Thank you, Mrs Bunting,' she said in a small voice.

'That's all right, my duck,' Mrs Bunting said softly. 'Just you eat up now.' She patted Maxy, just once, on the shoulder. Maxy smiled at her, then ate until her plate was clean.

Mrs Bunting and Maxy did the washing up, then it was time for Mrs B to go. Maxy stood at the door to say goodbye.

'Your dad'll be home in an hour,' said Mrs Bunting. 'So you stay inside, out of the weather, all right?' Maxy nodded. Mrs Bunting got in her car.

'I like your little chooks,' she said before she closed the door. 'Fresh eggs, that's just what your mum'll need when she comes home, to build up her strength. Shame she can't get them in that hospital, food's all out of a packet there. Bye now.' The car door slammed and Mrs Bunting clattered off down the lane.

Maxy stood in the quiet kitchen and stared at the two white eggs in the bowl. It was no good sending raw eggs to hospital, but hard-boiled ones would be OK. She took a small saucepan out of the cupboard and filled it with cold water, then she put the eggs in the water and set it on the range. She didn't know how long it took to hard boil eggs, so she left them bubbling away while she fetched her crayons and some paper.

Maxy drew a picture of the new coop, with Elvis, Coffee and Cream standing together in the run. Minerva was standing on top of the drinker with a massive wriggly worm in her beak. There was blue sky over the apple tree, and the sun was shining. Then she thought very hard about the Pretend Cows, and while she was thinking, she wrote, 'To Mum' very fast, at the top of the picture.

Maxy made a case for the eggs from an old egg box. She

crayoned patterns all over it and wrote 'hard boiled' in big letters on the lid.

When that was done, she took the pan off the stove and spooned the cooked eggs into the decorated egg box. For a moment she felt pleased, but then she noticed how lonely the two eggs looked in the box, with four empty spaces beside them. How much better they'd look with just one more egg, a very special little egg, from a very fierce little chicken! Maybe by now Minerva had laid an egg.

The wind was blowing hard, slapping the rain into Maxy's face as she crossed the yard. The weather had driven the chickens to roost already; none of them were out in the run. Maxy lifted the egg box lid a crack and felt about inside; no eggs, nothing but straw. She lifted the lid a little more, so she could look inside and be sure she hadn't missed a little egg. In the dimness of the roost Maxy saw Elvis was on the perch, with Cream under his left wing and Coffee under his right. She was just thinking how sweet this was, when Minerva popped out of the shadows. Her eyes were brighter than ever, and she moved quickly. Before Maxy had the chance to even think, the little chicken was out under the open lid, and into the air! She wasn't a very good flyer, and she had to flap very hard to move at all, but she managed to get up into the apple tree. Maxy could see her, high in the branches, clinging on tight in the wind and

already soaked and bedraggled by the rain. Maxy had to get her down! She was so tiny. How could she survive a night out in the storm?

She began to climb the apple tree, but the trunk was slimy with rain and wellies were no good for climbing. She was on her fourth try when Dad got home. He ran through the puddles towards her. Maxy could see he was very cross.

'How could you be so silly? Tree climbing in a storm! Get inside this instant!'

Back inside, Maxy explained about Minerva's escape. She didn't say anything about the third egg, but Dad saw the picture and the egg box on the table and stopped being so cross. He told her to have a hot bath and get ready for bed.

When she came down in her pyjamas, he hadn't got changed, ready to go to the hospital. He was still sitting at the table in his work clothes, looking at her picture.

'I thought I'd give the hospital a miss tonight,' he said. 'Mum'll be fine without me for an evening.'

Maxy looked at Dad's face. He was tired, but he wasn't scared. Maxy smiled at him. Maybe Mum really would be fine.

'Shall I take her your picture tomorrow night?' Dad asked quietly.

Maxy nodded. 'And the eggs,' she said.

'Yes, and the eggs,' said Dad.

The storm rattled the windows and buffeted the door. Dad made some hot chocolate and they sat sipping and listening to the wind racing around the yard. Maxy worried about Minerva.

'Will she be safe up the tree?'

'She'll be fine, don't you worry,' said Dad. 'And she'll be so hungry in the morning that she'll eat out of your hand.'

Maxy didn't believe him but she was too sleepy to argue.

Maxy was dreaming. She dreamt the storm had blown itself out and quiet moonlight streamed into her room from a clear, starry sky. Dad came in and sat on her bed. Even in the dark she could tell he was smiling and smiling.

'I have to go, Maxy,' he said. 'The baby's being born. It'll be here by the morning. Nan's come to sleep in the spare room.' Then he got up and left. Maxy filled up with a warm, lovely feeling that she couldn't name at first. Then she said to herself, 'It's happiness, that's what it is!'

So she lay on her dream bed, which was just like a real one, and felt very happy. She looked through the window at the moon sailing in the sky. The light was so bright. Outside there would be moon shadows, and everything would be lit up in blue and silver. The fields, the barns, the apple tree... and the little chicken asleep in its branches.

Maxy got up in her dream. Then she slipped downstairs and out into the yard.

Everything was as clear as day, shiny with the rain and glinting like glitter on a Christmas card. All the puddles were made of melted moonshine and every tiny pebble had been dipped in silver. She crossed the yard as quietly as she could and stood at the bottom of the apple tree, listening. There was only one sound: a faint purring from the chicken roost. Dream chickens purring in their sleep. Maxy smiled to herself and began to climb. It was still a bit slippery but easy to climb in bare feet.

She reached her favourite place, the Y where a big branch met the trunk. She looked up into the branches, all very white and very black in the moonlight. There was no sign of Minerva. Maxy stepped into the Y, ready to climb higher, and almost stepped on the tiny chicken. She had cuddled up to the trunk, just as Maxy had done so many times, and she was fast asleep with her head tucked under her wing. She didn't even stir when Maxy picked her up and tucked her safely inside her pyjama top for the climb down.

Maxy felt inside the roost for the warm fluffy shapes of Elvis and the silkies, then she put Minerva next to them on the perch, cuddled up cosy and safe. Just as Maxy let the little bantam go, she purred a tiny squeaky purr and snuggled deeper under her own wing.

Maxy tiptoed back across the yard, afraid to make a sound and somehow spoil the silent, silvery dreamworld. She went back to bed, curled up like a sleepy bantam and shut her eyes.

Maxy woke feeling funny. There was something she was supposed to remember but she couldn't think what it was. Was there a school trip today she'd forgotten about? Was it somebody's birthday, but she couldn't think who? It was light outside but the sky was still dawn-pink. Too early even for Dad to be up. She crept downstairs to look for clues.

The picture and the egg box had gone from the table. Maxy couldn't work out why. She got herself a drink of orange juice from the fridge and noticed that her hand left a dirty mark on the carton. She was filthy: hands, feet, pyjamas. It didn't make any sense... and then she remembered the feel of the wet bark under her bare feet. The glittery shininess of her midnight adventure shot through Maxy all at once like a silver arrow. She threw open the kitchen door and ran over the yard to the apple tree and chicken coop.

She was in a daze. The pink early morning sky and the moonlight glow of the night whirled around inside her, real and dream and pretend all mixed up together. She wanted it all to be true, the baby and Mum, and Minerva all safe; but maybe it was only as real as the Pretend Cows.

Elvis, Coffee and Cream were scratching in their little yard, but Minerva was nowhere to be seen. Maxy felt the tears prickling her eyes. She lifted the lid of the egg box a little and looked inside. Staring up at her, bold and fierce, was the little hen! She was sitting cosily in the straw, but when she saw Maxy she jumped up clucking and went out into the run. Maxy looked down at where Minerva had been sitting. There, beside the two fat little eggs, was a much smaller one, deep brown and speckled.

Maxy wanted to shout with happiness. She flew back to the house and fetched the quilt from her bed. Then she wrapped it around herself and sat down outside the kitchen door. All she had to do now was wait.

It didn't take long. At six o'clock Nan opened her bedroom curtains, and a moment later Dad's car pulled into the yard! Dad rushed towards Maxy and hugged her as if his life depended on it. Then Nan ran out of the kitchen in her dressing gown and hugged them both.

'You've got a baby brother!' Dad said to Maxy.

'And I've got a grandson,' said Nan.

'Is Mummy all right?' Maxy asked.

'Yes, love,' said Dad gently. 'Fine. Eating hard-boiled eggs when I left her!'

Maxy gave the biggest sigh.

'Can we go and see them?' asked Maxy.

Dad smiled a funny, rainy smile, his eyes full of tears.

'Yes, we can.'

'Just as soon as we've had breakfast!' said Nan.

'Good!' said Maxy. 'There's one egg each!'

Nicola Davies

Nicola is an award-winning author whose many books for children include *The Promise* (Green Earth Book Award 2015, CILIP Kate Greenaway Medal Shortlist 2015), *Tiny* (AAAS/Subaru SB&F Prize 2015), *A First Book of Nature*, *Whale Boy* (Blue Peter Book Awards Shortlist 2014), and the Heroes of the Wild series (Portsmouth Book Award 2014).

She graduated in Zoology, studied whales and bats and then worked for the BBC Natural History Unit. Underlying all Nicola's writing is the belief that a relationship with nature is essential to every human being, and that now, more than ever, we need to renew that relationship.

Nicola's children's books from Graffeg include *Perfect* (2017 CILIP Kate Greenaway Medal longlist), *The Pond* (2018 CILIP Kate Greenaway Medal longlist), the Shadows and Light series, *The Word Bird*, *Animal Surprises* and *Into the Blue*.

Cathy Fisher

Cathy Fisher grew up with eight brothers and sisters, playing in the fields overlooking Bath.

She has been a teacher and practising artist all her life, living and working in the UK, Seychelles and Australia.

Art is Cathy's first language. As a young child she scribbled on the walls of her bedroom and ever since has felt a sense of urgency to paint and draw stories which she feels need to be heard and expressed.

Cathy's first published book with Graffeg was *Perfect*, followed by *The Pond*, written by Nicola Davies. Both books were longlisted for the CILIP Kate Greenaway Medal.

Country Tales series by Nicola Davies

Flying Free
Nicola Davies
Illustrations by Cathy Fisher

The Little Mistake
Nicola Davies
Illustrations by Cathy Fisher

The Mountain Lamb
Nicola Davies
Illustrations by Cathy Fisher

A Boy's Best Friend
Nicola Davies
Illustrations by Cathy Fisher

Pretend Cows
Nicola Davies
Illustrations by Cathy Fisher

Spikes and Sam
Nicola Davies
Illustrations by Cathy Fisher

Visit our website author pages at www.graffeg.com for more about
Nicola Davies and illustrator Cathy Fisher, plus a complete list of our
children's books and merchandise.

Graffeg Children's Books

Perfect
Nicola Davies
Illustrations by Cathy Fisher

The Pond
Nicola Davies
Illustrations by Cathy Fisher

The White Hare
Nicola Davies
Illustrated by Anastasia Izlesou

Mother Cary's Butter Knife
Nicola Davies
Illustrations by Anja Uhren

Elias Martin
Nicola Davies
Illustrations by Fran Shum

The Selkie's Mate
Nicola Davies
Illustrations by Claire Jenkins

Bee Boy and the Moonflowers
Nicola Davies
Illustrations by Max Low

The Eel Question
Nicola Davies
Illustrations by Beth Holland

Pretend Cows
Published in Great Britain in 2020
by Graffeg Limited

Written by Nicola Davies
copyright © 2020.
Illustrated by Cathy Fisher
copyright © 2020.
Designed and produced by Graffeg
Limited copyright © 2020.

Graffeg Limited, 24 Stradey Park
Business Centre, Mwrwg Road,
Llangennech, Llanelli, Carmarthenshire,
SA14 8YP, Wales, UK.
Tel 01554 824000 www.graffeg.com

ISBN 9781912654123

1 2 3 4 5 6 7 8 9